More Adventures
of the
Wishing-Chair

Enid Blyton

More Adventures of the Wishing-Chair

DRAGON
Granada Publishing

Dragon Books
Granada Publishing Ltd
8 Grafton Street, London W1X 3LA

Published by Dragon Books 1974
Reprinted 1976, 1978, 1979, 1981, 1983, 1984

First published in 1937
The complete volume published by
Dean & Son Ltd 1971
This edition contains the last fourteen
chapters from the complete edition of
Adventures of the Wishing-Chair.
The first twelve chapters are published
by Dragon Books under the title
Adventures of the Wishing-Chair.

ISBN 0-583-30198-3

Printed and bound in Great Britain by
Collins, Glasgow

Set in Linotype Baskerville

CONTENTS

Chapter		Page
1	The Polite Goblin	9
2	The Spinning House	16
3	Witch Snippit	22
4	The Silly Boy	30
5	The Windy Wizard	36
6	Mr Twisty	44
7	Two Bad Children	51
8	The Horrid Quarrel	57
9	The Enchanter Clip-Clap	65
10	The Strange Tower	72
11	The Great Escape	80
12	Big-Ears the Goblin	88
13	The Snoogle	95
14	The Snoogle's Castle	103

Publisher's note
about THE WISHING-CHAIR

The Wishing-Chair, Mollie, Peter, and Chinky the Pixie all make their first appearance in THE ADVENTURES OF THE WISHING-CHAIR (also available in Dragon):

Mollie and Peter are looking for a birthday present for their mother in a strange old shop when a most extraordinary thing happens:

'The chair they were in began to creak and groan, and suddenly it rose up in the air, with the two children in it! They held tight, wondering whatever was happening! It flew to the door, but that was shut. It flew to the window, but that was shut too ...

The chair finding that it could not get out of the door or the window, flew up the little stairway. It nearly got stuck in the doorway at the top, which was rather narrow, but just managed to squeeze itself through. Before the children could see what the room upstairs was like, the chair flew to the window there, which was open, and out it went into the street. It immediately rose up very high indeed, far beyond the housetops, and flew towards the children's home. How amazed they were! And how tightly they clung to the arms! It would be dreadful to fall!

'I say, Mollie, can you hear a flapping noise?' said Peter. 'Has the chair got wings anywhere?' Mollie peeped cautiously over the edge of the chair. 'Yes!' she said. 'It has a little red wing growing out of each leg, and they make the flapping noise! How queer!'

The chair began to fly downwards. The children saw that they were just over their garden.

'Go to our playroom, chair,' said Peter quickly. The chair went to a big shed at the bottom of the garden. Inside was a playroom for the children, and here they kept all their toys and books, and could play any game they liked. The chair flew in at the open door and came to rest on the floor. The children jumped off and looked at one another.

'The first real adventure we've ever had in our lives!' said Mollie, in delight. 'Oh, Peter, to think we've got a magic chair – a wishing-chair!'

In their very first adventure Mollie and Peter, with the help of the Wishing-Chair, rescue Chinky, a little pixie, from the evil clutches of a big bad giant. Chinky becomes their faithful friend and accompanies them on many of their exciting adventures.

Now read on....

CHAPTER ONE

THE POLITE GOBLIN

The next time the chair grew its wings again, Chinky looked at it sternly.

'Last time you were very badly behaved!' he said. 'If you want us to come with you this time, just behave yourself. If not, I'll sell you to the Jumble-Man, and you won't like that!'

The chair flapped its wings violently, and Chinky grinned at the others. 'That will make it behave itself this time,' he said. 'It wouldn't like to be given to the Jumble-Man! Come on, let's get in.'

They all got in. The chair rose very slowly, and flew out of the door, taking care not to jerk or jolt the children at all. It flew so very slowly and carefully that Chinky got quite impatient.

'Now you're being silly!' he said to the chair. 'Do fly properly. You're hardly moving.'

The chair flew faster. It flew very high and the children could hardly see the houses below them. They even flew above the clouds – and suddenly, to the children's great astonishment, they saw a big castle built on a cloud!

'I say! Look!' said Peter, in amazement. 'A

castle on a cloud! Who lives there, Chinky?'

'I don't know,' said Chinky. 'I hope it's someone nice. I don't want to meet a giant this morning!'

The chair flew to the castle. There was a big front door standing open. The chair flew inside.

'Goodness!' said Mollie, in alarm. 'This isn't very polite. We ought to have knocked!'

The chair came to rest in a big kitchen. A small goblin, with pointed ears, green eyes, and bony legs and arms, was sitting in a chair reading a paper. When the wishing-chair flew in with Chinky, Mollie, and Peter in it, he jumped up in astonishment.

The children and Chinky got out of their chair. 'Good-morning,' said Chinky. 'I'm sorry to come in like this – but our chair didn't wait to knock.'

The goblin bowed politely. 'It doesn't matter at all!' he said. 'What a marvellous chair you have, and how pleased I am to see you! Pray sit down and let me give you some lemonade!'

They all sat down on stools. The goblin rushed to a cupboard and brought out a big jug of lemonade.

'It is nice to see such pleasant visitors,' said the goblin, putting a glass of lemonade before each of them. 'And now, will you have biscuits?'

'Thank you,' said Mollie and Peter and Chinky. They felt that it was kind of the goblin to welcome them – but they didn't like him at all. He seemed *much* too polite!'

'Another glass of lemonade?' asked the goblin, taking Chinky's empty glass. 'Oh do! It is a pleasure, I assure you, to have you here! Another biscuit, little girl? I make them myself, and only save them for *special* visitors.'

'But we aren't very special,' said Peter, thinking that the goblin was really silly to say such things.

'Oh yes, you are *very* special,' said the goblin, smiling politely at them all. '*So* good of you to come and see an ugly little goblin like me!'

'But we didn't *mean* to come and see you,' said Mollie truthfully. Chinky frowned at her. He

didn't want her to offend the goblin. He did not
trust him at all. He wanted to get away as soon as
he could.

'Well,' said Chinky, finishing his biscuit, 'it is
kind of you to have welcomed us like this. But now
we must go.'

'Good-bye and thank you,' said the polite goblin.
He shook hands with each of them and bowed very
low. They turned to go to the wishing-chair.

And then they had a most *terrible* shock! The
wishing-chair was not there! It was gone.

'I say! Where's the wishing-chair?' shouted
Chinky. 'Goblin, where's our chair?'

'Oh, pixie, how should *I* know?' said the goblin. 'Haven't I been looking after you every minute? It must have flown away when you were not looking.'

'Well, it's funny if it has,' said Chinky. 'We should have seen it, or at least felt the wind of its wings flapping. I don't believe you, goblin. You have done something with our chair – your servants have taken it away! Tell me quickly, or I will punish you!'

'*Punish* me!' said the goblin. 'And how would you do that, pray? You had better be careful, pixie – how are you going to get away from my castle without a wishing-chair? I live here by myself in the clouds!'

'Be careful, Chinky,' said Peter. 'Don't make him angry. Goodness knows how we'd escape from here if he didn't help us!'

Mollie looked frightened. The little goblin smiled at her politely, and said, 'Don't be afraid, pretty little girl. I will treat you as an honoured guest for as long as you like to stay with me in my castle.'

'We don't want to stay with you at all,' said Chinky. 'We want our wishing-chair! What have you DONE with it?'

But he could get no answer from the polite goblin. It was most tiresome. What in the world were they to do?

Chinky suddenly lost his temper. He rushed at

the goblin to catch him and shake him. The goblin looked scared. He turned to run and sped out of the big kitchen into the hall. Chinky ran after him. Mollie and Peter looked at one another.

'Chinky will get us all into trouble,' said Mollie. 'He really is a silly-billy. If he makes the goblin angry, he certainly won't help us to get away. I suppose that naughty wishing-chair flew away home.'

'I'm quite sure it didn't,' said Peter. 'I know I would have seen it moving.'

The goblin came running into the room followed by Chinky. 'Catch him, catch him!' yelled Chinky. Peter tried to – but the goblin was like an eel. He dodged this way, he dodged that way – and then a funny thing happened. Peter fell over something that wasn't there!

He crashed right into something and fell over, bang! And yet, when he looked, there was nothing at all to fall over! He felt very much astonished. He sat up and stared round. 'What did I fall over?' he said. Chinky stopped chasing the goblin and ran to him. He put out his arms and felt round about in the air by Peter – and his hands closed on something hard – that couldn't be seen!

'Oh!' he yelled joyfully, 'it's the wishing-chair! That deceitful goblin made it invisible, so that we couldn't see it, even though it was really here! And he meant to help us home all right – and as soon as we had gone he meant to use our wishing-chair for himself, and we'd never know!'

'Then it hasn't flown away!' cried Mollie running over and feeling it too. 'Oh goody, goody! We can get into it and go home even if we can't see what we're sitting on! Get up, Peter, and let's fly off before that nasty little polite goblin does any more spells!'

They all sat in the chair they couldn't see. 'Home, wishing-chair, home!' cried Chinky. The invisible chair rose in the air and flew out of the door. The goblin ran to the door and bowed. 'So pleased to have seen you!' he called politely.

'Nasty little polite creature!' said Chinky. 'My goodness – we nearly lost the chair, children! Now we've got to find a way of making it visible again. It's no fun having a chair and not knowing if it's really there or not! I don't like feeling I'm sitting on nothing! I like to *see* what I'm sitting on!'

They flew home. They got out of the chair and looked at one another.

'Well, we do have adventures!' said Peter, grinning.

CHAPTER TWO

THE SPINNING HOUSE

It was most annoying not being able to see the wishing-chair. The children kept forgetting where it was and falling over it.

'Oh dear!' groaned Peter, picking himself up for the fourth time, 'I really can't bear this chair being invisible. I keep walking into it and bumping myself.'

'I'll tie a ribbon on it!' said Mollie. 'Then we shall see the ribbon in the air, and we'll know the chair is there!'

'That's a good idea,' said Chinky. 'Girls always think of good ideas.'

'So do boys,' said Peter. 'I say! How queer that ribbon looks all by itself in the air! We can see it, but we can't see the chair it's tied on! People *would* stare if they came in here and saw it!'

It certainly did look funny. It stuck there in mid-air – and it did act as a warning to the children and Chinky that they must be careful not to walk into the invisible chair. It saved them many a bump.

'I've been asking the fairies how we can get the chair made visible again,' said Chinky the next day.

'They say there is a funny old witch who lives in a little spinning house in Jiffy Wood, who is very, very clever making things invisible *or* visible! So if we fly there the next time the chair grows wings, we may be able to have it put right.'

'But how shall we know when it grows its wings if we can't see them?' said Mollie.

'I never thought of that!' said Chinky.

'I know!' said Peter. 'Let's tear up little bits of paper and put them round the legs of the chair on the floor! Then, when its wings grow, the bits will fly about in the draught the wings make with their flapping – and we shall see them and know the chair is ready to go off adventuring again!'

The children tore up the bits of paper and put them on the floor near the legs of the chair.

'Really, it does look funny!' said Mollie. 'A ribbon balanced in mid-air – and bits of paper below, on the floor! Mother would think us very untidy if she came in.'

'Let's play tiddly-winks now,' said Peter. 'I'll get out the cup and the counters.'

Soon the three of them were playing tiddly-winks on the floor. Mollie flipped her counters into the cup very cleverly, and had just won, when Chinky gave a shout:

'Look! Those bits of paper are fluttering into the air! The chair must have grown its wings!'

Mollie and Peter turned to look. Sure enough,

the scraps of paper they had put on the floor were all dancing up and down as if a wind was blowing them. The children could feel a draught too, and knew that the wishing-chair had once again grown its red wings.

'That was a good idea of yours, Peter,' said Chinky. 'Boys have good ideas as well as girls, I can see! Come on, let's get into the chair and see if it will fly to Jiffy Wood to the old witch's.'

They climbed on to the chair. It was really very strange climbing on to something they couldn't see, but could only feel. Chinky sat on the back, as usual, and the children squeezed into the seat.

'Go to Jiffy Wood, to the little Spinning House,' Chinky said to the chair. It rose up into the air, flew out of the door, and was up high before the children could say another word! They must have looked very queer, sitting in a chair that couldn't be seen!

It was raining. Mollie wished they had brought an umbrella. 'Tell the chair to fly above the clouds, Chinky,' she said. 'It's the clouds that drop the rain on to us. If we fly beyond them, we shan't get wet because there won't be any rain.'

'Fly higher than the clouds, chair,' said Chinky. The chair rose higher and higher. It flew right through the misty grey clouds and came out above them. The sun was shining brightly! It made the other side of the clouds quite dazzling to look at!

'This is better,' said Mollie. 'The sun will dry our clothes.'

They flew on and on in the sunshine, above the great white clouds. Then they suddenly flew downwards again, and the children saw that they were over a thick wood.

'Jiffy Wood!' said Chinky, peering down. 'We shall soon be there!'

Down they flew and down, and at last came to a little clearing. The chair flew down to it, and came to rest on some grass. A little way off was a most peculiar house. It had one leg, like a short pole, and it spun round and round and round on this leg! It did not go very fast, and the children could see that it had a door on one side and a window on each of the other three sides. It had one chimney which was smoking away merrily – but the smoke was green, a sign that a witch lived in the house.

'Well, here we are,' said Chinky, getting out of the chair. 'I'd better carry the chair, I think. I don't like leaving it about here when we can't see it. We shouldn't know where it was if any one came along and untied the ribbon.'

'Is the old witch a fierce sort of person?' asked Mollie.

'No, she's a good sort,' said Chinky. 'She will do all she can to help us, I know. You needn't be afraid. She won't harm us. My grandmother knew her very well.'

'How are we going to get into the house?' asked Peter, looking at the strange house going round and round and round. 'It's like getting on a round-about that's going! Our mother always says that's a dangerous thing to do.'

'Well, we'll try and get the witch to stop the house spinning round for a minute, so that we can hop in with the chair,' said Chinky. 'Come on. I've got the chair.'

Off they went towards the queer little house. As it went round the smoke went round too, and made green rings. It was very peculiar.

'Witch Snippit, Witch Snippit!' called Chinky. 'Stop your house and let us in!'

Some one opened a window and looked out. It was an old woman with a red shawl on and a pretty white cap. She had a hooky nose and a pair of large spectacles over her eyes. She seemed surprised to see them.

'Wait a minute!' she called. 'I'll stop the house. But you'll have to be very quick getting in at the door because it won't stop for long!'

The house slowed down – it went round more and more slowly – and at last it stopped. The door was facing the children, and the witch opened it and beckoned to them. Mollie shot inside, and so did Peter. Chinky was trying to get in, with the chair too, when suddenly the house began to spin round fast again! Poor Chinky fell out of the doorway with the chair!

Mollie and Peter really couldn't help laughing, he looked so funny! The witch stopped the house again, and then Peter helped Chinky in quickly. They put the wishing-chair down and then turned to greet the witch.

'Good-morning,' she said, with a nice smile. 'And what can I do for you?'

CHAPTER THREE

WITCH SNIPPIT

The children and Chinky looked at the smiling witch. They liked her very much. She had kind blue eyes, as bright as forget-me-nots. At first they felt rather giddy, for the house they were in spun round and round all the time – but they soon got used to it.

'We've brought our wishing-chair to you,' said Chinky. 'We went to the cloud-goblin's castle the other day, and he made our chair invisible. It's such a nuisance to have a chair we can't see – so as we knew you were clever at all kinds of visible and invisible spells, we thought we would bring it to you. Could you make our chair seeable please?'

'Certainly,' said Witch Snippit. 'I have some very strong magic paint. If you use it, you will make your chair easily seen.'

She went to the cupboard. The children stared round the room.

It was a very strange room indeed. The clock on the mantlepiece had legs, and for every tick it gave, it walked a step along the mantlepiece.

When it got to the end it turned and walked back again. Then it suddenly disappeared!

'Ooh!' said Mollie, surprised. Your clock's gone, Witch Snippit!'

'Oh, don't take any notice of that,' said the witch. 'It's just showing off!'

The clock said 'Urrrrrrrrr!' and came back again. Up and down it walked, and the children thought it was the strangest one they had ever seen.

Other things in the cottage were most peculiar too. There was a chair that had four legs and a back, but no seat. Mollie wondered if it really *had* got a seat that couldn't be seen. She went to sit down on it and found that it *had* got a seat, but it was quite invisible. There was a table, too, that had a top but no legs.

On the dresser there were cups with no handles, and lids balanced in the air but no dishes below. Mollie put out her hand and felt the dishes, but she couldn't see them. She turned round to Witch Snippit.

'You *have* got a funny home,' she began – and then she stopped in surprise. Witch Snippit was all there except her middle! Oh dear, she did look so funny!

'Don't be worried,' she said to Mollie. 'I'm quite all right. My middle is really there, but it's vanished for a few minutes. You can't meddle about with visible and invisible magic without having things like this happen to you at times.'

As she spoke, her middle came back again, and, oh dear, her hands and feet went! Mollie began to laugh. 'Whatever will go next!' she said.

All of the witch disappeared then – and the children and Chinky couldn't see her anywhere! They knew she was in the room, because they could hear her laughing.

'Don't look so surprised,' she said. 'You should never be astonished at anything that happens in a witch's house.'

'I say! The floor's gone!' said Peter, in alarm, looking down at his feet. 'Oooh! I feel as if I'm falling! Where's the floor?'

'Oh, it's there all the time,' said Witch Snippit,

coming back in bits. 'It's only disappeared from sight. Don't worry, it's there!'

She put a tin of paint on the table. 'Would *you* like to paint your chair and get it right again?' she asked. 'It's quite easy. There are three brushes for you. It's good paint. It will make invisible things visible, or visible things *in*visible. I'm rather busy to-day, so if you'll do the job yourself, I'll be glad.'

'We'd love to!' said Chinky. He took off the lid of the paint tin and picked up a brush. 'It's going to be funny painting something you can't see!' he said.

He felt for the legs of the chair and dipped his brush into the paint, which was a queer silvery colour and seemed as thin as smoke. He painted along one of the chair's invisible legs – and hey presto! it came into sight, as brown and solid as ever!

'I've got a leg back!' said Chinky, in excitement, and waved his brush in the air. A drop of paint flew on to Peter's nose.

'Don't,' said Peter. Mollie stared at him in horror. His nose had disappeared!

'Peter, your nose has gone!' she said. 'A drop of the paint went on to it! Oh, whatever shall we do?'

'Get it back again, of course,' said Chinky. 'Didn't you hear Witch Snippit say that this paint acted either way? It makes things seen that can't be seen, and it makes things that are seeable *un*-seeable! Come here, Peter – I'll paint where your nose should be, and it'll come back again!'

He dabbed some paint where he thought Peter's nose should be – and sure enough, it *did* come back again! Mollie was so glad. Peter looked horrid without a nose.

'I'll teach you to make my nose disappear!' said Peter to Chinky. He dipped his brush in the paint and dabbed at Chinky's pointed ears. They vanished in a trice.

'Don't!' said Chinky crossly. He threw some paint at Peter's feet and they disappeared at once!

'Oh!' said Peter, surprised. 'I don't like having no feet. I shall paint them back! There they are! Stop it, Chinky. I don't like this game. It would be awful if something *didn't* come back!'

Chinky was naughty. He dipped his brush in the magic paint, and ran it round Mollie's neck. How queer she looked with a head and a body but no neck! Peter couldn't bear it. He painted her neck in again at once, and frowned at Chinky.

'If you're not careful I'll paint you from top to toe and then take away the tin of paint!' he said.

'Now listen to me,' suddenly said Witch Snippit's voice above them. 'I didn't give you that paint to waste. If you are not careful there will not be enough to finish painting your wishing-chair, and then you will find there is a bit still left invisible, that you cannot see. So be sensible.'

Chinky and Peter went red. They began to paint the chair busily, and Mollie joined them. The clock on the mantelpiece was so interested in what they were doing that it walked right off the mantelpiece and fell into the coal-scuttle.

'It can stay there,' said the witch. 'It is much too curious – always poking its nose where it isn't wanted.'

'Urrrrrrrrr!' said the clock, and disappeared. Mollie was glad her clock at home didn't behave like that.

In an hour's time the wishing-chair was itself again, and all the paint in the tin was finished. There it stood before them, their same old wishing-chair. It had been very strange to see it gradually becoming visible to their eyes.

'There's a bit at the back here that can't be seen,' said Mollie, pointing to a bit that hadn't come back again. But there was no paint to finish that bit, and the children didn't like to ask for any more. So that tiny piece of the chair had to remain invisible. It looked like a hole!

'Thank you very much, Witch Snippit,' said Chinky politely. 'We've finished now, and had better be getting home. Could you stop your house spinning and let us go out?'

'Very well,' said Witch Snippit. She called out a magic word and the spinning house slowed down.

'Good-bye,' she said to Chinky and the children. 'Come and see me again another time. Hurry, now, or the house will start spinning again!'

The three squeezed into the wishing-chair. The house stopped and the witch opened the door.

'Home, wishing-chair!' shouted Chinky – and the chair flew straight out of the door and up into the air.

'Good-bye, good-bye!' called Mollie and Peter, looking down at the house, which was already spinning fast again. 'I say, that was a pretty good adventure, wasn't it!'

'I wish we'd got some of that magic paint with

us,' said Chinky. 'We could have some fun with it!'

'I'm glad we haven't!' said Mollie. 'I don't know *what* mischief you'd get into, Chinky!'

CHAPTER FOUR

THE SILLY BOY

The children were cross because Mother had said that the painters were to paint the walls of the playroom and mend a window – and this meant that they couldn't play there for some time.

Their playroom was built right at the bottom of the garden, and it was quite safe for their friend, Chinky, the pixie, to live there, for no one ever went to the garden playroom except themselves. But now the painters would be there for a week. How tiresome!

'It's a good thing it's summer-time, Chinky, so that you can live in the garden for a bit,' said Mollie.

'Oh, don't worry about *me*,' said Chinky. 'I've a nice cosy place in the hollow of an oak tree. It's the chair I'm thinking about. Where shall we keep that? We can't have it flying about whilst the painters are there.'

'We'd better put it in the boxroom, indoors,' said Peter. 'That room's just been repainted so don't expect Mother or any one will think it ust be turned out just yet. It will be safe there.'

, when no one was looking, Peter and Mollie

carried the wishing-chair up to the boxroom and stood it safely in a corner. They shut the window up tightly, so that it couldn't fly out if its wings grew suddenly.

They couldn't have Chinky to play with them in the house, because he didn't want any one to know about him. So they asked Thomas, the little boy over the road, to come and play soldiers, on a rainy afternoon.

They didn't like him very much, but he was better than nobody.

Thomas came. He soon got tired of playing soldiers. He began turning head-over-heels down the nursery floor. He could do it very well.

'I can make awful faces, too,' he said to Mollie and Peter – and he began to pull such dreadful faces that the two children gazed at him in surprise and horror.

'Our mother says that if you pull faces and the wind happens to change you may get stuck like that,' said Mollie. 'Do stop it, Thomas.'

But Thomas wouldn't. He wrinkled up his nose and his forehead and blew out his cheeks – and do you know, the wind changed that very minute! And poor Thomas couldn't get his face right again! he tried and he tried, but he couldn't. It was dreadful! Whatever was he to do?

'Oh, Thomas, the wind changed – I saw the weather-cock swing round that very moment!'

cried Mollie. 'I did warn you! I do think you're silly.'

'He can't go home like that,' said Peter. 'Let's wash his face in hot water – then perhaps it will go right again.'

So they washed Thomas's face well – but it was as bad as ever when they had finished! Screwed-up nose and forehead and blown-out cheeks ... oh dear!

'Do you suppose Chinky would know what to do?' said Peter at last.

'Who's Chinky?' asked Thomas.

'Never you mind,' said Mollie. 'Peter, go and find Chinky and see what he says. I'll stay here with Thomas. He mustn't go out of the nursery, because if he meets Mother or Jane, they will think he's making faces at them and will be ever so cross.

Peter ran downstairs. He went into the garden and whistled a little tune that Chinky had taught him. He had to whistle this whenever he wanted the pixie.

Chinky whistled back. Peter saw him under a big hawthorn bush, mending a hole in his coat.

'What's up?' asked Chinky, sewing away.

'We've got a boy in our nursery who's been making dreadful faces,' explained Peter. 'And the wind changed just as he was making a specially horrible one – and now he can't get his face right

again. So Mollie sent me to ask you if you could do anything to help.'

'A boy as silly as that doesn't deserve help,' said Chinky, breaking off his cotton and threading his needle again. 'You go and tell him so.'

'Oh no, Chinky, we really *must* help him,' said Peter. 'His mother may think *we* made his face like that, and we'll get into trouble. You don't want us to be sent to bed for a week, do you?'

'No, I don't,' said Chinky, putting on his coat. 'I'll help *you* because you're my friends. There's only one thing to be done for a person who's been making faces when the wind changed.'

'What's that?' asked Peter.

'You've got to get a bit of the wind that blew just then, and puff it into his face,' said Chinky. 'Then he'll be all right – but it's dreadfully difficult to get a bit of the same wind.'

'How can we?' asked Peter, in dismay.

'We'd better go in the wishing-chair to the Windy Wizard,' said Chinky. 'He knows all the ins and outs of every wind that blows. I've seen the old wishing-chair looking out of the window this afternoon, trying to get out, so I'm sure it's grown its wings again. Go and see, and if it has, tell Mollie, and we'll go and get help from the old wizard.'

'Oh, thank you, Chinky,' said Peter, and he ran indoors. He whispered to Mollie all that Chinky had said.

'I think the chair *must* have grown its wings,' Mollie said, 'because there have been such queer sounds going on in the boxroom this afternoon – you know, knockings and bumping. I expect it's the chair trying to get out.'

'I'll go and see,' said Peter. He ran up the topmost flight of stairs and opened the boxroom door. The wishing-chair was standing by it, ready to fly out – but Peter caught hold of it just as it was slipping out of the door.

'Now just wait a minute,' he said. But the chair

wouldn't! It forced its way past Peter and the little boy jumped into it. 'Go to Chinky!' he called hoping that the chair wouldn't meet any one on the way.

The chair flew down the stairs and out into the garden. It went to where Chinky was standing by the hawthorn bush. It was flapping its red wings madly and Chinky jumped into it at once.

'To the Windy Wizard's!' he shouted. 'I say, Peter, isn't it in a hurry! It must have got tired of being shut up in the boxroom!'

Mollie was looking out of the window. She had heard the chair flying downstairs. She saw it up in the air, carrying Peter and Chinky, and she wished she were in it too!

'Some one's got to stay with Thomas, though,' she thought to herself. 'He'd only run home or go and find our mother or something, if we left him quite alone. What an ugly face he has now! I do hope Peter and Chinky find something to put it right!'

CHAPTER FIVE

THE WINDY WIZARD

The wishing-chair rose high into the air, carrying Peter and Chinky. It had stopped raining and was a hot sunny day and the wind the chair made rushing through the air was very pleasant. Peter wished Mollie was with them. It was much more fun to go on adventures all together.

Presently the chair came into a very windy sky. Goodness, how the wind blew! It blew the white clouds to rags. It blew Peter's hair nearly off his head! It blew the chair's wings so that it could hardly flap them.

'The Windy Wizard lives somewhere about here,' said Chinky, looking down. 'Look! Do you see that hill over there, golden with buttercups? There's a house there. It's the Windy Wizard's, I'm sure, because it's rocking about in all directions as if the wind lived inside it!'

Down flew the wishing-chair. It came to rest outside the cottage, which was certainly rocking about in a most alarming manner. Peter and Chinky jumped off and ran to the cottage door. They knocked.

'Come in!' cried a voice. They opened the door

and went in. Oooh! The wind rushed out at them and nearly blew them off their feet!

'Good-day!' said the Windy Wizard. He was a most peculiar-looking person, for he had long hair and a very long beard and a cloak that swept to the ground, but, as the wind blew his hair and beard and cloak up and down and round and about all the time, it was very difficult to see what he was really like!

'Good-day,' said Peter and Chinky, staring at the wizard. He hadn't a very comfortable house to live in, Peter thought, because there were draughts everywhere, round his legs, down his neck, behind his knees! And all the cottage was full of a whispering, sighing sound as if a wind was talking to itself all the time.

'Have you come to buy a little wind?' asked the wizard.

'No,' said Chinky. 'I've come about a boy who made faces when the wind changed – and he can't get right again. So we thought perhaps you could help us. I know that if we could get a little of the wind that blew at that time, and puff it into his face, he'll be all right – but how can we get the wind?'

'What a foolish boy!' said the Windy Wizard, his cloak blowing out and hiding him completely. 'What time did this happen?'

'At half-past three this afternoon,' said Peter.

'I heard the nursery clock strike.'

'It's difficult, very difficult,' said the wizard, smoothing down his cloak. 'You see, the wind blows and is gone in a trice! Now let me think for a moment – who is likely to have kept a little of that wind?'

'What about the birds that were flying in the air at that moment?' asked Chinky. 'They may have some in their feathers, you know.'

'Yes, so they may,' said the wizard. He took a feather from a jar that was full of them, and flung it out of the door.

> 'Come, birds, and bring
> The breeze from your wing!'

he chanted.

Peter and Chinky looked out of the door, hoping that dozens of birds would come – but only one appeared, and that was a blackbird.

'Only one bird was flying in the air with the wind at that moment,' said the wizard. 'Come, blackbird, shake your feathers. I want the wind from them!'

The blackbird shook his glossy feathers out and the wizard held a green paper bag under them to catch the wind in them. The bag blew up a little, like a balloon.

'Not enough wind here to change your friend's

face back again!' said the wizard, looking at it.
'I wonder if there were any kites using the wind at
that moment!'

He went to a cupboard and took the tail of a kite
out of it. He threw it up into the air just outside
the door.

> 'Come, kites, and bring
> The breeze from your wing!'

he called.

Peter and Chinky watched eagerly – and to their
delight saw two kites sailing down from the sky.
One was a green one and one was a red. They fell

at the wizard's feet.

He shook each one to get the wind into his green bag. It blew up just a little more.

'Still not enough,' said the wizard. 'I'll get the little ships along. There will surely be enough then!'

He ran to the mantelpiece and took a tiny sailor doll from it. He threw it up into the air and it disappeared.

'Come, ships, and bring
The breeze from your wing!'

sang the old wizard, his hair and beard streaming out like smoke.

Then, sailing up a tinkling stream that ran down the hillside came six little toy sailing ships, their sails full of the wind. They sailed right up to the wizard's front door, for the stream suddenly seemed to run there – and quickly and neatly the old wizard seized each ship, shook its sails into the green paper bag, and then popped it back on the stream. Away sailed the ships again and Peter and Chinky saw them no more.

The paper bag was quite fat and full now.

'That's about enough, I think,' said the wizard. 'Now I'll put the wind into a pair of bellows for you!'

He took a small pair of bellows from his fireside and put the tip of them into the green paper bag. He opened the bellows and they sucked in all the air from the bag. The wizard handed them to Peter and Chinky.

'Now don't puff with these bellows until you reach your friend,' he said. 'Then use them hard and puff all the air into his face! It will come right again in a twink!'

'Thank you so much for your help,' said Chinky gratefully. He and Peter ran to the wishing-chair again and climbed into it, holding the bellows carefully. The chair rose up into the air as Chinky cried, 'Home, chair, home!'

In a few minutes it was flying in at the boxroom window, for Mollie had run up and opened it, ready for the chair when it came back again. Peter and Chinky shut the window after them, ran down to the nursery and burst in at the door.

Thomas was still there, his face screwed up and his cheeks blown out!

'I'm so glad you're back!' said Mollie. 'It's horrid being here with Thomas. His face is so nasty to look at, it makes me feel I'm in a dream! Have you got something to make it right?'

'Yes,' said Chinky, showing her the bellows. 'The Windy Wizard has filled these bellows full of the wind that blew when Thomas made that face. If we puff it at him, his face will be all right again!'

'Go on then, puff!' said Mollie. So Chinky lifted up the bellows and puffed them right into Thomas's face – phoooooof! Thomas gasped and spluttered. He shut his eyes and coughed – and when he opened them, his face had gone right again! His nose and forehead were no longer screwed up, and his cheeks were quite flat, not a bit blown up!

'You're right again now, Thomas,' said Chinky. 'But let it be a lesson to you not to be silly any more.'

'I'll never pull faces again,' said Thomas, who had really had a dreadful fright. 'But who are you? Are you a fairy?'

'Never mind who I am, and don't say a word about me or what has happened this afternoon!'

said Chinky, and Thomas promised. He ran home feeling puzzled, but very happy to think that he had got his face its right shape again.

'Well, that was an exciting sort of adventure, Mollie!' said Peter, and he told her all about it. 'The Windy Wizard was *so* nice. I say – what about giving him back his bellows?'

'I'll manage that,' said Chinky, taking them. 'I must go now or some one will come into the nursery and see me! Good-bye till next time!'

CHAPTER SIX

MR. TWISTY

One day, when the two children and Chinky were in their playroom at the bottom of the garden, reading quietly, a knock sounded at the door.

They looked up. A small man stood there, with his straw hat in his hand and a sly look on his face.

'Have you anything old to sell?' he asked. 'I buy old clothes, furniture, carpets – anything you like. I'll give you a good price for it too.'

'No, thank you,' said Mollie. 'We couldn't sell anything unless our mother said so.'

'What about that old chair there?' said the man, pointing to the wishing-chair. 'It can't be wanted or you wouldn't have it in your playroom. I like the look of that. I'll give you a good price for that.'

'Certainly not!' said Peter. 'Please go away, or I'll call the gardener.'

The little man put on his straw hat, grinned at them all, and went. Chinky looked uncomfortable. 'I don't like the look of him,' he said to the children. 'He may make trouble for us. I think I'll hop out into the garden to-day. I don't like people seeing me here.'

So he hopped out and went to play with the fairy

folk there – and a good thing he did too – for in
about ten minutes Mother came down the garden
followed by the little man in the straw hat.

'Are you there, Peter and Mollie?' she said. 'Oh,
this man, Mr. Twisty, says he will buy anything
old – and he saw an old chair here he would like to
buy. I couldn't remember it – which is it?'

Poor Mollie and Peter! They had kept their
wishing-chair such a secret – and now the secret
was out! They really didn't know what to say.

Mother saw the chair and looked puzzled. 'I don't remember that chair at all,' she said.

'I'll give you two pounds for it,' said Mr. Twisty. "'Tisn't worth it – but I'll take it for that.'

'That seems a lot of money for a playroom chair,' said Mother. 'Well, fetch it to-night, and you can have it.'

'Oh, Mother, Mother!' shrieked the two children in despair. 'You don't understand. It's our own, very own chair. We love it. It's a very precious sort of chair.'

'Whatever do you mean?' said Mother, in surprise. 'It doesn't look at all precious to me.'

Well, Mollie and Peter knew quiet well that they couldn't say it was a wishing-chair and grew wings. It would be taken away from them at once, then, and put into a museum or something. Whatever were they to do?

'Two pounds for that dirty old chair,' said Mr. Twisty, looking slyly at Mother.

'Very well,' said Mother.

'I'll send for it to-night,' said Mr. Twisty, and he bowed and went off up the garden path.

'Don't look so upset, silly-billies!' said Mother. 'I'll buy you a nice comfy wicker-chair instead.'

Mollie and Peter said nothing. Mollie burst into tears as soon as Mother had gone. 'It's too bad!' she sobbed. 'It's our own wishing-chair – and that horrible Mr. Twisty is buying it for two pounds.'

Chinky came in, and they told him what had happened. He grinned at them, and put his arm round Mollie. 'Don't cry,' he said. 'I've got a good plan.'

'What?' asked Mollie.

'I can get Mr. Knobbles, the pixie carpenter who lives out in the field over there, to make me a chair almost exactly like the wishing-chair!' said Chinky. 'We'll let Mr. Twisty have that one – not ours! He won't know the difference. He doesn't know ours is a wishing-chair – he just thinks it's an old valuable chair. Well, he can buy one just like it – without the magic in it!'

'Ooh!' said Mollie and Peter, pleased. 'Can you really get one made in time?'

'I think so,' said Chinky. 'Come along with me and see.'

So they squeezed under the hedge at the bottom of the garden and crossed the field beyond to where a big oak tree stood. Chinky pulled a root aside, that stuck out above the ground, and under it was a trap-door!

'You simply *never* know where the little folk live!' said Mollie excitedly.

Chinky rapped on the door. It flew up and a bald-headed pixie with enormous ears popped his head out. Chinky explained what he wanted and the pixie invited them into his workshop underground. It was a dear little place, scattered

47

with small tables, chairs, and stools that the carpenter had been making.

'Do you think you could make us the chair in time?' asked Mollie eagerly.

'Well, if I could get a quick-spell, I could,' said the pixie. 'A quick-spell makes you work three times as fast as usual, you know. But they are so expensive.'

'Oh,' said Mollie and Peter, in dismay. 'Well, we've hardly any money.'

'Wait!' said Chinky, grinning at them in his wicked way. 'Remember that Mr. Twisty is paying two pounds for the chair! Can you make the chair and buy the quick-spell for two pounds, Mr. Knobbles?'

Mr. Knobbles worked out a sum on a bit of paper and said he just could. He came back to the playroom with the children and saw their own chair. He nodded his head and said he could easily make one just the same. The children were so pleased. They hugged Chinky and said he was the cleverest person they had ever known. He always knew just how to get them out of any difficulty.

'Now, we'd better hide our own chair,' said Chinky. 'Where shall we put it?'

'In the gardener's shed!' said Mollie. 'Gardener will be gone at five. We'll put it there, then.'

So they did, and covered it up with sacks. Just as they came back from the shed, they met Mr.

Knobbles carrying on his back a new chair, just *exactly* like their old one! It was marvellous!

'The quick-spell worked quickly!' he said. 'Here's the chair. You can bring me the money any time.'

The children thanked him and put the chair in their playroom. Then they waited for Mr. Twisty.

He turned up for it at half-past six, his straw hat in his hand, and the usual wide smile on his sly face. 'Ah, there's the chair!' he said. 'Here's the money! Thank you very much!'

He took the chair on his back, paid over the money and went, whistling a tune.

'Well, he's got a marvellous pixie-chair for his money,' said Chinky, 'but he hasn't got a wishing-chair! He can sell that chair for twenty pounds, I should think – for Mr. Knobbles has made it beautifully – hasn't used a single nail – stuck everything with magic glue!'

'And *we've* got our own dear chair still!' cried the two children, and sat down in it for joy.

Just then Mother popped her head in – and saw the chair! Chinky only *just* had time to hide himself behind the sofa!

'Why!' she said, 'the chair isn't sold after all! I'm quite glad, because it really is a pretty chair. I can't imagine how I came to let you have it in your playroom. I think I will have it in the house. Bring it up with you to-night, Peter.'

Mother went away again. Chinky popped out from his hiding-place and looked at the others in dismay.

'I say!' he said. 'That's bad news. You'll have to do as you're told, Peter. Take the chair up to the house with you when you go to-night – and we'll try and think of some way out of this new fix. Oh dear! Why can't we have our own chair!'

So Peter took it up to the house with him – and Mother put it into the study. Suppose it grew wings there! Whatever would happen?

CHAPTER SEVEN

TWO BAD CHILDREN

Mollie and Peter were very upset. Mother had got their wishing-chair in the study – and if it grew its wings there the grown-ups might see them – and then their great secret would be known. Whatever could be done about it?

Chinky had no ideas at all. He simply didn't know how to get the chair back into the playroom. If they just took it back, Mother would notice and would have it brought to the house again.

Peter and Mollie thought very hard how to get the chair for their own again – and at last Mollie had an idea. She and Peter ran down to the playroom to tell Chinky.

'This is my idea,' said Mollie. 'It's a very naughty one and we shall get into trouble – but I don't see how we can help it. After all, it *is* our chair!'

'Go on, tell us your plan,' said Peter.

'It's this,' said Mollie. 'Let's spill things over the chair – and tear the seat or something – and scratch the legs! Then, when Mother sees how dirty and scratched and torn it is, she won't think it is good enough for the study – and perhaps we can have it back again!'

'I say! That's a really good idea!' said Peter and Chinky together.

'But we *shall* get into trouble!' said Peter. 'You know how Mother hates us to mess things – that's why we have this playroom at the bottom of the garden – so that we can do as we like and not spoil things in the dining-room or drawing-room or study up at the house.'

'Well, even if we do get into trouble it will be worth it if we can get back our chair,' said Mollie. 'I don't mind being punished if we can only go for some more adventures.'

'All right,' said Peter. 'I don't either. What shall we do first?'

'We'll spill some ink across the seat,' said Mollie.

'Come on, then,' said Peter. So they shouted good-bye to Chinky, who wished them good luck, and ran up to the house. They went into the study. The wishing-chair stood there, looking very good and proper. Mother had put a fine new cushion into it. Mollie took it out. She didn't want to spoil anything that belonged to Mother.

Peter got the ink-bottle, and the two children emptied ink across the seat of the chair. Then they went to tell Mother.

She *was* cross! 'How very, very careless of you!' she scolded. 'You shall not go out to tea to-day, Peter and Mollie. I am very much annoyed with you. It's a good thing the ink didn't get on to my new cushion.'

Mollie and Peter said nothing. They did not go out to tea that day, and they were sad about it – but they kept thinking that perhaps they might get their wishing-chair back – so they did not get too unhappy.

The next day Peter sat in the wishing-chair and kicked his boots against the legs as hard as he could, so that they were scratched and dented. Mother heard him kicking and put her head into the study to see what was going on there.

'Peter!' she cried, 'why aren't you out in the garden on this fine day – and do stop kicking your feet against that chair! Oh, you bad boy, see what you have done!'

She ran over to the chair and looked at the legs. They *were* scratched!

'This is very naughty, Peter,' said Mother. 'Yesterday you and Mollie spilt ink on this chair – and now you have kicked it like this. You will go to bed for the rest of the day!'

Poor Peter! He went very red, but he marched upstairs without a word. It was horrid to have to be so careless with a chair, especially one he loved so much – but still, somehow or other he *had* to get it back to the playroom! Suppose it grew its wings when Mother was sitting in it and flew away with her. Whatever would she do? She would be so frightened!

Mollie was sorry that Peter had been sent to bed. She crept into his room and gave him a piece of chocolate to eat.

'I'm going to slit the seat now,' she whispered. 'I expect I'll be sent to bed too – but surely after that Mother will say the chair isn't good enough for the study and we'll have it back again!'

So Mollie went downstairs, and took her work-basket into the study. She got out her scissors and began to cut out some dolls' clothes – and then, oh dear, she ran her scissors into the seat of the chair and made a big cut there!

Mother came in after a while – and she saw the slit at once. She stared in horror.

'Mollie! Did you do that?'

'I'm afraid I did, Mother,' said Mollie.

'Then you are as bad as Peter,' said Mother crossly. 'Go to bed too. This chair is simply dreadful now – inky, torn, and scratched! It will have to go back to the playroom. I can't have it in the study. You are two bad children, and I am ashamed of you both.'

It was dreadful to have Mother so cross. Mollie cried when she got into bed – but she was comforted when she thought that the wishing-chair was really going back to the playroom. She and Peter had to stay in bed all day, and they were very tired of it. But when the next day came, they carried the chair back to their playroom and called Chinky.

'We've got the chair, Chinky!' they cried. 'Hurrah! But we did get into trouble. We both went to bed for the day, and Mother was dreadfully cross. We shall have to be extra nice to her now to make up – because we didn't really mean to vex her. Only we *had* to get the chair back somehow!'

'Good for you!' said Chinky, pleased. He looked at the chair and grinned.

'My word!' he said. 'You did do some damage to it, didn't you! What a mess it's in! Mollie, you'd better get your needle and cotton and mend the seat – and Peter and I had better polish up the legs a bit and try and hide the scratches!'

So that morning the children and Chinky worked hard at the chair and by dinner-time it really looked very much better. Mollie put back into it the cushion they always had there, and then clapped her hands for joy.

'Dear old wishing-chair!' she said. 'It's nice to have you again! Mr. Twisty nearly got you – and Mother nearly had you too – but now we've got you back again at last!'

'And *I'm* longing for another adventure!' said Peter. 'I wish it would grow its wings again!'

'It soon will!' said Chinky. 'I expect it wants another adventure as much as we do!'

CHAPTER EIGHT

THE HORRID QUARREL

One morning Mollie, Peter, and Chinky were playing in the playroom at the bottom of the garden. It had been raining all morning, which was horrid in the summer-time. The children and the pixie were very tired of staying indoors.

They had played ludo and snap and draughts and snakes-and-ladders and dominoes. Now there didn't seem any other game to play, and they were getting cross and bored.

'Cheer up, Peter!' said Mollie, looking at Peter's cross face. 'You look like a monkey that's lost its tail.'

'And you look like a giraffe with a sore throat,' said Peter rudely.

'Don't be horrid!' said Mollie.

'Well, don't you, then,' said Peter.

'I'm not,' said Mollie.

'You are,' said Peter.

'Now be quiet, you two,' said Chinky. 'I don't like to hear you quarrelling. You only get silly.'

'Don't interfere,' said Peter crossly. 'You talk too much, Chinky.'

'Yes, remember we've been given two ears but

57

only one mouth – so you should talk only half as much as you hear,' said Mollie.

'Same to you,' said Chinky. 'All girls talk too much.'

'They *don't*!' said Mollie. 'How horrid of you to say that, Chinky.'

'You're horrid this morning, too,' said Chinky. 'You're both horrid.'

'Well, if you think that, just go away and play somewhere else,' said Mollie at once. '*We* don't want you!'

'All right then, I will!' said Chinky, offended – and to the children's dismay he got up and walked out of the playroom!

'There! Now see what you've done!' said Peter, getting up. 'Sent Chinky away! Suppose he doesn't come back!'

He ran to the door and called. 'Chinky! Hie, Chinky! Come back a minute!'

But there was no answer. Chinky had gone. There was no sign of him anywhere.

'I do think you are horrid and silly,' said Peter to Mollie. 'Fancy sending Chinky away like that!'

'I didn't mean to,' said Mollie, almost in tears. 'He was being horrid, so I was too. We were all being horrid.'

'*I* wasn't,' said Peter.

'Yes, you were,' said Mollie.

'No, I wasn't,' said Peter.

'Yes, you were,' said Mollie. 'I shall smack you in a minute.'

'Now, now!' said a voice, and Mother looked in at the door. 'You are silly to quarrel like that! Uncle Jack is here and wants to know if you would like to go with him to the farm. They have some puppies there, and he wants to choose one for himself. Would you like to go and help him?'

'Oh yes!' cried Peter and Mollie. 'We'll put on our macs and rubber boots and go with him!'

So off they ran, forgetting all about their quarrel – and all about Chinky too! They went to the farm with Uncle Jack and chose a lovely black puppy with him. Then back home they went, chattering and laughing, forgetting all about how horrid they had been, and enjoying their lovely walk.

It was dinner-time when they got home. They had dinner and ran down to the playroom afterwards, meaning to ask Chinky to play with them in the field outside the garden.

But Chinky wasn't in the playroom. Peter and Mollie looked at one another and went red.

'Do you suppose he has *really* gone?' said Mollie, feeling upset.

'I don't know,' said Peter. 'I'll whistle for him outside and see if he comes trotting out of the bushes!'

So Peter went to the door and whistled the little

pixie tune that Chinky had taught him. But no Chinky came trotting up. It was really horrid.

'Suppose he never, never comes again!' said Mollie, crying. 'Oh, I do, do wish I'd never said that to him – telling him to go away. I didn't really mean it.'

'I shan't like going on adventures in the wishing-chair unless Chinky is with us,' said Peter. 'It isn't any fun without him.'

'Peter, do you suppose he will *never* come and see us again?' asked Mollie.

'I shouldn't be surprised,' said Peter. 'Pixies are funny, you know – not quite like ordinary people.'

The two children would have been very unhappy indeed if something hadn't suddenly happened to take their minds away from their disappointment. The wishing-chair suddenly grew its wings again!

'Look!' said Mollie excitedly. 'The chair is ready to fly off again. Shall we go, Peter?'

'I don't feel as if I want to, now Chinky's not here,' said Peter gloomily.

'But, Peter, I've such a good idea!' said Mollie, running to him. 'Listen! Let's get in the wishing-chair and tell it to go to Chinky's home, wherever it is. I expect he's gone back there, don't you? Then we can say we're sorry and ask him to come back again.'

'That's a fine idea,' said Peter, at once. 'Come

on, Mollie. Get in! We'll go at once.'

So the two children squeezed into the wishing-chair. It had grown its four red wings round its legs and was lazily flapping them to and fro, longing to be off into the air once more.

'Go to Chinky's home,' commanded Peter. The chair rose up into the air, flew out of the door and rose high above the trees. It was fun to fly again. The two children looked down on the gardens and fields, and wished Chinky were with them, sitting in his usual place on the top of the chair!

'I wonder where Chinky's home *is*,' said Peter. 'He has never told us.'

'We shall soon see,' said Mollie.

The chair flew on and on, just below the clouds. Soon it came to the towers and spires of Fairyland. Then it suddenly flew downwards to a little village of quaint crooked houses, all of them small, and all of them with bright flowery gardens. The chair flew down into one of the gardens and rested there. The children jumped off at once.

They went to the little red door of the house and knocked.

'Won't Chinky be surprised to see us!' said Mollie.

The door opened. An old pixie woman, with a very sweet face and bright eyes, looked out at them.

'Oh!' said Mollie, in disappointment. 'We thought this was Chinky's home.'

'So it is when he is at home!' said the pixie woman. 'I'm his mother. Come in, please.'

They went into a neat and spotless little kitchen. Chinky's mother set ginger buns and lemonade in front of them.

'Thank you,' said Peter. 'Do you know where Chinky is?'

'He came and asked me to make up his bed for to-night,' said the pixie woman. 'He said he had quarrelled with you, and wanted to come and live at home again.'

The children went red. 'I didn't mean what I said,' said Mollie, in a little voice.

'I expect Chinky was to blame too,' said his mother. 'He went out to buy himself a new hand-kerchief – and though I've been waiting and wait-ing for him he hasn't come back – so I wondered if he had gone back to you again.'

'No, he didn't come back,' said Peter. 'I wonder what's happened to him. We'll stay a little while, if you don't mind, and see if he comes back.'

Chinky didn't come back – but in a short while a round, fat pixie came running up the path and into the kitchen, puffing and panting.

'Oh, Mrs. Twinkle!' he cried, when he saw

Chinky's mother. 'A dreadful thing has happened to Chinky!'

'What!' cried everyone in alarm.

'He had bought himself a nice new red hand-kerchief and was walking down the lane home again when a big yellow bird swooped down from the air, caught hold of Chinky by the belt, and flew off with him!' cried the pixie.

'Oh my, oh my!' wept Mrs. Twinkle. 'I know that bird. It belongs to the enchanter Clip-clap. He always sends that bird of his out when he wants to capture some one to help him. Poor Chinky!'

'Don't cry!' said Peter, putting his arm round the old woman. 'We'll go and look for Chinky. The magic chair we have will take us. We will try to bring him back safely. It's a very good thing we came to look for him! Come on, Mollie – get into the wishing-chair and we'll tell it to go wherever Chinky is!'

In they both got. Peter told the chair to go to Chinky, and it rose into the air.

'Another adventure!' said Mollie. 'I do hope it turns out all right!'

CHAPTER NINE

THE ENCHANTER CLIP-CLAP

The wishing-chair rose high up and flew steadily towards the west. It had a long way to go so it flew faster than usual, and all its four wings flapped swiftly.

'I wonder where the enchanter lives,' said Mollie. 'I hope he won't capture us too!'

'Well, all this would never have happened if we hadn't quarrelled with Chinky,' said Peter. 'He wouldn't have gone back home then—and wouldn't have gone out to buy a new handkerchief — and wouldn't have been captured by the yellow bird that swooped down on him and took him away!'

'I shall never quarrel again,' said Mollie. It made her very sad when she remembered the unkind things she had said that morning.

The chair flew over a wood. Mollie leaned over the arm of the chair and looked down.

'Look, Peter,' she said. 'What is that funny thing sticking out of the wood?'

Peter looked. 'It's a very, very high stone tower,' he said. 'Isn't it strange? It's just a tower by itself. It doesn't seem to be part of a castle or anything. I say! The chair is flying down to it! Do you suppose that is where the enchanter lives?'

'It must be,' said Mollie. The children looked eagerly downwards to see what sort of tower this was. It certainly was queer. It had a pointed roof but no chimneys at all. The chair circled all round it as it flew downwards, trying to find a window. But there was not a single window to be seen!

'This really is a very magic sort of tower!' said Mollie. 'Not a window anywhere! Well, there must be a door at the bottom to get in by.'

The chair flew to the ground and stayed there. The children jumped off. They went to the tower and looked for the door. There was not one to be seen!

The tower was quite round, and very tall indeed, higher than the highest tree – but it had no doors and no windows, so it seemed quite impossible to get into it. Mollie and Peter walked round and round it a great many times, but no matter how they looked, they could see no way to get in.

'Do you suppose Chinky is in there,' said Mollie at last.

'Sure to be,' said Peter gloomily. 'We told the chair to take us to where Chinky was, you know.'

'Well, what are we going to do?' asked Mollie. 'Shall we call for Chinky loudly?'

'No,' said Peter at once. 'If you do that the enchanter will know we are here and may capture us too. Don't do anything like that, Mollie.'

'Well, how else are we to tell Chinky we are here?' said Mollie. 'We must *do* something, Peter. It's no good standing here looking for doors and windows that aren't there.'

'Sh!' said Peter suddenly, and he pulled Mollie behind a tree. He had heard a noise.

Mollie caught hold of the wishing-chair and pulled that behind the tree too – and only just in time!

There came a loud noise, like the clip-clapping of thunder. A great door appeared in the round tower, half as high as the tower itself. It opened – and out came the enchanter Clip-clap! He was very tall and thin, and he had a long beard that reached the ground. He wore it in a plait and it looked very queer.

'See you finish that spell properly!' he called to some one in the tower. Then there came another loud clapping noise, just like a roll and crash of thunder, and the door in the tower closed – and vanished! The enchanter strode away through the wood, his head almost as high as the trees!

'Goodness!' said Mollie. 'We only just got behind this tree in time. It's impossible to get into that tower, Peter. We should never know how to make that door appear.'

'What *are* we to do!' sighed Peter. 'I hate to think of poor old Chinky a prisoner in there – and all because we quarrelled with him, too.'

'Let's hide the chair under a bush and see if we can find any one living near here,' said Mollie.

'We might find someone who can help us.'

So they carefully hid the chair under a bramble-bush, and piled bracken over it too. Then they found a little path and went down it, wondering where it led to.

It led to a small and pretty cottage. The name was on the gate ... Dimple Cottage. Mollie liked the sound of it. She thought they would be quite safe in going there.

They knocked. To their enormous surprise the door was opened by a brown mouse! She wore a check apron and cap, and large slippers on her feet. The children stared. They could never get used to this sort of thing, although they had seen many strange sights by now.

'Good-afternoon,' said Peter, and then didn't know what else to say.

'Do you want to see my mistress?' asked the mouse.

'Well, yes, perhaps it would be a good idea,' said Peter. So the mouse asked them in and showed them into a tiny drawing-room.

'What are we going to *say*?' whispered Peter – but before Mollie had time to answer, some one came into the room.

It was a small elf, with neat silvery wings, silvery golden hair, and a big dimple in her cheek when she smiled. Mollie and Peter liked her at once.

'Good-afternoon,' she said. 'What can I do for you?'

Both talking at once, the two children told her their troubles – how they had quarrelled with Chinky – and he had gone home – and been caught by the yellow bird belonging to the enchanter Clip-clap – and how their wishing-chair had brought them to the strange tower.

'But we don't know how to get into it and we are afraid of being caught by Clip-clap too,' said Peter. 'I don't know if you can help us?'

'I don't think I can,' said the elf, whose name was Dimple. 'No one knows a spell powerful enough to get into the enchanter's tower. I've lived here for three hundred years and no one has ever got into that tower except the enchanter and his servants and friends. I wouldn't try if I were you.'

'We *must*,' said Mollie. 'You see, Chinky is our own friend – and we must help him.'

'Yes – we have to help our friends,' said the elf. 'Wait a minute – I wonder if my mouse knows anything that might help us. Harriet! Harriet!'

The little servant mouse came running in. 'Yes, Madam,' she said.

'Harriet, these children want to get into the enchanter's tower,' said Dimple. 'Do you know of any way in?'

'Well yes, Madam, I do,' said Harriet.

'Oh, do you!' cried Mollie, in delight. 'Do, do tell us, Harriet!'

'My auntie lives down in the cellars of the tower,' said the little mouse. 'Sometimes, on my afternoon off, I go to see her.'

'And how do you get into the tower?' asked Dimple.

'Down the mouse-hole of course,' said Harriet. 'There's one on the far side of the tower. I always scamper down there.'

'Oh,' said the children, in disappointment, looking at the small mouse. '*We* couldn't get down a mousehole. We are too big. You are a big mouse, but even so, the mouse-hole would not take us!'

Mollie was so disappointed that she cried into her handkerchief. Dimple patted her on the back.

'Don't do that,' she said. 'I can give you a spell to make you small. Then you can slip down the mouse-hole with Harriet, and see if you can find Chinky.'

'Oh thank you, thank you!' cried the children, in delight. 'That *is* kind of you!'

Dimple went to a shelf and took down a box. Out of it she took two pills. They were queer because they were green one side and red the other!

'Here you are,' she said. 'Eat these and you will be small enough to go down the hole. They taste horrid, but never mind.'

The children each chewed up a pill. They certainly had a funny taste – but they were very magic indeed, and no sooner were they eaten than Mollie and Peter felt as though they were going down in a lift – for they suddenly grew very tiny indeed! They looked up at Dimple, and she seemed enormous to them!

'Harriet, take off your apron and cap and take these children to your auntie,' said Dimple. So Harriet carefully folded her cap and apron and then went out with the children. She took them to the tower and showed them a small hole under the wall.

'Down here!' she said – and down they all went!

CHAPTER TEN

THE STRANGE TOWER

The hole was dark and smelt a bit funny. Mollie clung tightly to Peter's hand. It was strange being so small.

Harriet the mouse went on in front, and they could see her little gleaming eyes as she turned round now and again. Once Peter trod on her tail and she gave an angry squeal.

'So sorry,' said Peter. 'I keep forgetting you have such a long tail, Harriet.'

At last they came to a place where the tunnel widened out into a room. It was very warm there. A large mouse pounced on Harriet and gave her a hug.

'Oh, Auntie, you're at home!' said Harriet. 'See, I've brought you two children. They wanted to get into the tower, so I thought they might as well use our mouse-tunnel. It's the only way in.'

'Good-afternoon,' said Harriet's aunt. She seemed just an ordinary mouse except that she wore large spectacles. Her home was chiefly made of paper, it seemed. There were hundreds of little bits of it, neatly made into beds and tables.

'What are the children going to do?' said Harriet's aunt.

'We would like to know how to get into the cellars,' said Peter. 'You see, if you show us the way there we can get into the tower above and perhaps find the friend we are looking for.'

'Well, come this way then,' said the aunt. 'But look out for the cat, won't you? She sometimes waits about in the cellar and you don't want her to catch you.'

She took them down another narrow passage, and then the children found themselves walking out of a hole into a dark, damp cellar.

'Good-bye,' said the mouse. 'I'll put a little candle just inside this hole, so that you will know the way back, children. I hope you find your friend.'

Mollie took Peter's hand. The cellar was very dark. A chink of light came from somewhere to the right.

'The cellar steps must go up towards that chink of light,' said Peter. 'Come on. Walk carefully in case we bump into anything. And look out for the cat! We are very small, you know.'

They found the steps. They seemed very, very big to the children, now that they were so tiny, and Peter had to help Mollie up each one. At last they got to the top. They looked under the door that stood at the top of the steps. Beyond was a kitchen.

'Do you suppose the enchanter is back yet?' whispered Mollie.

'No,' said Peter. 'We should have heard that clip-clapping noise if he had come back. I think we are safe at the moment. But we must hide at once if we hear him coming. And look out for the cat, Mollie.'

'Can we squeeze under the door, do you think?' asked Mollie. But they couldn't. The crack was not big enough. However, the door was not quite closed, and by pushing with all their might the two children managed to get just enough open to squeeze through.

They looked round. They were in a very big kitchen – or it seemed big to them, because they were so tiny. They could not see Chinky anywhere.

'Come on,' said Peter, giving Mollie his hand. 'We'll go into the next room.'

'Meow!' suddenly came a voice, and a large tabby cat with green eyes came out from behind a chair. Mollie felt quite shaky at the knees. She knew what a mouse must feel like when it saw a cat! What a giant of an animal it seemed!

'Don't show it you are frightened,' said Peter. 'It has smelt us, and we don't smell like mice. Stay here a moment, Mollie, and I'll go over to it and stroke what I can reach of it.'

'Oh, Peter, you *are* brave!' said Mollie. Peter walked boldly over to the cat and stroked her legs. She seemed very pleased and purred loudly. Peter beckoned to Mollie. She ran over and stroked the cat too. It was a friendly creature.

It went into the next room, purring to Mollie and Peter, who followed her. This room was very small and was lighted by a candle. No daylight came into the tower, for there were no windows.

No one was in this little room either. A dish stood on the floor with some milk in it, and a large round basket with a fat cushion in it stood nearby.

'This must be the cat's room,' said Mollie. 'There is no furniture in it. I do wonder where Chinky is.'

There were some stairs going upwards from the cat's little room. The children climbed them with great difficulty for they were very small, and the stairs seemed very big.

Before they got to the top they heard the sound of crying. It was Chinky! He must indeed be very unhappy if he were crying! He hardly ever cried.

How Mollie and Peter tried to climb those stairs quickly! At last they reached the top and found themselves before a big open door. They ran in. Chinky was lying on a small bed, crying as if his heart would break!

'Chinky! Chinky! Don't cry! We are here to rescue you!' shouted Peter, hoping that Chinky would hear his voice, for it was a very small one now.

Chinky did hear it. He sat up at once, with the tears still running down his cheeks. He saw Mollie and Peter and stared at them in surprise.

'Chinky!' cried Mollie, running over to him. 'We've come to save you. Cheer up! We got in through a mouse-hole after an elf had made us small. How can we save you?'

'Oh, you are good, good friends to come and look for me,' said Chinky, drying his eyes. 'I hate being here. I hate this enchanter. He wants me to do bad spells, and I won't. I was afraid I would be here for hundreds of years and never see you again.'

'Tell us how we can get away,' said Peter.

'Well, the only way in seems to be the mouse-hole you came by,' said Chinky. 'So I suppose the only way out is the mouse-hole too. But I'm too big to go that way.

'Well, I'll go back to Dimple's cottage and ask her for a pill to make you small like us,' said Peter, at once. 'Then when I bring it back you can take it, and we'll all go down the hole, get Dimple to make us the right size again, find the wishing-chair, and go home. See?'

'It sounds easy enough,' said Chinky. 'But I don't somehow think it will all go quite so nicely as that. Still, we can but try. Leave Mollie here with me, Peter, and you go down the mouse-hole again.'

'We'll see him safely to the cellar door,' said Mollie. So they all went down the stairs again, and were just going through the cat's little room when Chinky turned pale.

'The enchanter's coming back!' he said. 'Oh, where can you hide?'

'Quick, quick, think of somewhere!' cried Mollie. There came a clip-clapping noise, like thunder, as she spoke. The tower split in half and a door came. It opened, and in strode the enchanter, tall and thin, his plaited beard sweeping the ground.

But before he had seen the two children Peter had pulled Mollie over to the cat's basket. The big cat was lying there comfortably. The children scrambled in and lay down by the cat, hiding in her thick fur. Chinky was left by himself.

'I smell children!' said the enchanter.

'How could children get into your tower, master,' said Chinky with a look of surprise.

The enchanter sniffed and began to look all round the two rooms. The cat did not stir. Clip-clap stroked her as he passed, and she purred – but she stayed in her basket, and Mollie and Peter cuddled close into her fur, hoping she would not move at all.

The enchanter did not think of looking in the cat's basket. He soon gave up the hunt and ran up the stairs, calling to Chinky to go with him.

'Go quickly now, Peter,' whispered Chinky, before he followed Clip-clap. 'Mollie can stay with the cat. She is safe there.'

Quick as could be Peter slipped across the floor to the cellar door, squeezed through the small opening, and made his way down the steps. He saw the tiny candlelight burning at the entrance to the mouse-hole and ran across to it. In he went and made his way up to the mouse-room. Harriet the mouse was still there, talking to her auntie.

'Please, will you take me back to Dimple?' asked Peter. 'It is very important.'

Harriet gave him her paw and took him up the hole out into the open air again. Then they hurried together to Dimple's cottage. Soon Peter had told

Dimple all that had happened. She gave him another red-and-green pill, and warned him to be careful not to let Clip-clap see him.

Then off went Peter to the mouse-hole again. Ah! Chinky would soon be safe!

CHAPTER ELEVEN

THE GREAT ESCAPE

Peter hurried from Dimple's cottage, holding the pill in his hand that was to make Chinky as small as he was — then they could all escape down the mouse-hole!

He ran down the hole and made his way to the cellar. He climbed up the steps to the kitchen. He peeped under the door. There was no one in the kitchen.

He ran over the floor to the little room belonging to the cat. The big grey tabby was still in the basket, and Mollie was there too, hiding safely under the thick fur. Good!

'Chinky is still upstairs with the enchanter,' she whispered. Just at that moment there came footsteps down the stairs, and the enchanter came in.

The cat jumped out of her basket and went to greet him, rubbing against Clip-clap's legs and purring loudly. Mollie and Peter crouched down in the basket and tried to hide under the cushion — but alas! The enchanter saw them!

'Aha! I *thought* I sniffed children!' he said. He came over to the basket and looked down.

'How small you are!' he said. 'I did not know

there were such small children to be found. What have you got in your hand, little boy?'

Oh dear! What Peter was holding so tightly was the little green-and-red pill that was to make Chinky small enough to go down the mouse-hole! Peter put his hand behind his back and glared at the tall enchanter.

But it was no use. He had to show Clip-clap what he had – and no sooner did the enchanter see the little green-and-red pill than he guessed what it was for!

'Oho!' he said. 'So you made yourselves small first, did you – and came in through a mouse-hole, I guess – thinking to make Chinky small too, so that he might escape the same way! Well – I'll spoil all that! You shall grow big again – and you won't be able to creep down *any* mouse-holes! You can stay here and help Chinky work for me!'

He tapped Mollie on the head and then Peter. They shot up to their own size again, and stared at Clip-clap in alarm and dismay. What a horrid ending to all their plans! They had thought themselves so clever, too.

'Well,' said Clip-clap, looking at them. 'You won't escape in a hurry now, I promise you! No one knows the secret of making the door come in this tower but me! Chinky! Chinky! Come and see your fine friends now!'

Chinky came running down the stairs and stopped in the greatest dismay when he saw Peter and Mollie, both their right size, standing in front of the enchanter.

'So you had all laid fine plans for escape, had you?' said Clip-clap. 'Well, now you can just settle down to working hard for me, and using those good brains of yours for my spells! Go and help Chinky to polish my bedroom floor, and after that you can clean all the silver wands I use for my magic!'

The three went upstairs very sadly and in silence. Chinky handed each child a large yellow duster and all three went down on their hands and knees and began to polish the wooden floor.

'Don't say a word till we hear Clip-clap go out again,' whispered Chinky. 'He has ears as sharp as a hare's.'

So nobody said a word until they heard the clip-clap crashing noise, and knew that the enchanter had gone out again. Then they stood up and looked at one another.

'What *are* we to do now?' groaned Peter.

'Listen!' said Chinky quickly. 'I have a plan. Where's the wishing-chair?'

'Under a bramble bush outside the tower,' said Peter. 'But what's the good of that? We can't get out to it, and certainly the chair can't get in!'

'I'm not so sure of that!' said Chinky. 'You know that mouse you told me about – Dimple's servant?

Well, if you could speak to her, Peter, and tell her to go to Dimple and tell her what's happened, she might be able to make the wishing-chair small enough for Harriet to get it down the mouse-hole and into the cellar. *I* know a spell to make it the right size – and then, when Clip-clap does his disappearing act and goes out through the tower door, we'll fly out too! See?'

'Oh Chinky, Chinky, you *are* clever!' cried Mollie, in delight. 'Peter, go down to the cellar and call Harriet. She may be somewhere about. If not, her auntie will surely be there!'

So Peter hurried down to the cellar and called Harriet.

She wasn't there, but her auntie came – the brown mouse with spectacles on. Peter told her all that had happened, and begged her to go and tell Dimple, the elf. She hurried off at once, and Peter waited anxiously to see what would happen next.

But Clip-clap came back before anything else had happened. He set the three to work polishing his magic wands – but took the magic out of them first! He wasn't going to have Chinky doing any magic with them, not he!

After tea Clip-clap went out again, and Peter hurried down to the cellar. To his great delight he found Harriet there – and just inside the mouse-hole she had their wishing-chair! It was as small as a doll's house chair.

'My auntie told me all that had happened,' whispered Harriet. 'I told Dimple, my mistress, and we found the wishing-chair. Dimple made it small enough for me to take down the mouse-hole. Here it is. Good luck!'

She pushed the tiny wishing-chair out of the hole.

Peter picked it up gladly and ran up the cellar-steps with it. How glad Chinky and Mollie were to see it!

'Now,' said Chinky, 'I must make it big again,'

He felt in his pockets and took out a duster coloured yellow and green. It had a queer-smelling polish in the middle in a great smear. Chinky began to polish the chair as hard as he could.

As he polished it, it grew bigger – and bigger – and bigger! The children watched in amazement.

At last it was its usual size. 'Where shall we hide it?' asked Mollie.

'I say! Don't let's hide it anywere!' said Peter suddenly. 'What about us all getting into it, and waiting till Clip-clap comes back? Then as soon as he opens the door to come in, we'll yell to the chair to fly out – and off we'll go! The enchanter won't know what's happening till it's too late to stop us!'

'That's a splendid idea!' said Chinky, at once. 'We'll do it. Come on – get in, you two – the enchanter may be in at any moment! We must be ready!'

'The good old wishing-chair still has its wings,' said Mollie, thankfully. 'Wouldn't it be awful if they went, and we couldn't fly away?'

'Don't say things like that in front of the chair,' said Peter. 'You know how silly it can be sometimes. Have you forgotten the time it landed us all into a chimney?'

''Sh!' said Chinky. 'I can hear Clip-clap coming.'

Crash! The tower split in two, and a great door appeared in the split. It opened – and in strode Clip-clap, calling Chinky. 'Hi, Chinky, Chinky!'

'Home, wishing-chair, home!' yelled Chinky. 'Hallo, Clip-clap – here I am!'

The chair rose up into the air, flew past the left ear of the astonished enchanter and shot out of the door before Clip-clap could shut it! They were safely out in the wood again!

'There's Dimple and Harriet below, waving like mad!' said Peter. 'Wave back, you two!'

They all waved to Dimple and Harriet and called good-bye. 'We'll send them a postcard when we get back,' said Chinky. 'They were very good to help us.'

'Won't Clip-clap be angry to think we've escaped after all!' said Mollie.

'I say! Oughtn't you to go and tell your mother you are safe?' said Peter. 'She was very worried about you.'

'I'll got to-night when you are both in bed,' said Chinky. 'I'll take you home safely first. My, what adventures we've had since this morning!'

'I'm not going to quarrel ever again,' said Mollie, as the chair flew in at the playroom door. She jumped off and flung her arms round Chinky. 'It was horrid when you didn't come back. I didn't mean what I said. You will always be our friend, won't you, Chinky?'

'Of course,' said Chinky, grinning all over his cheeky pixie face. 'I would have come back the next day. I was just in a bad temper. We all were.'

'I'm sorry about it, too,' said Peter. 'Anyway, we're all together again, friends as much as before.'

'You'd better run in and show your mother you're all right,' said Chinky. 'Mothers are such worriers, you know. You've not been in to tea, so yours will wonder if you're all right. Good-bye! Thanks so much for rescuing me.'

Peter and Mollie ran off happily.

Thank goodness everything was all right again! Good old wishing-chair – what *would* they do without it?

CHAPTER TWELVE

BIG-EARS THE GOBLIN

One day, when Mollie and Peter were playing with Chinky in the playroom, they heard footsteps running down the garden.

'Quick! Hide, Chinky! There is some one coming!,' cried Mollie. The pixie always hid when any one was about. He ran to a cupboard and got inside. Peter shut the door just as Mother came into the playroom.

'Children!' she said, I've lost my ring! I must have dropped it in the garden somewhere. Please look for it, and see if you can find it.'

Peter and Mollie were upset. They knew that their mother was very fond of her best ring. It was a very pretty one, set with diamonds and rubies. They ran out into the garden and began to hunt – but no matter where they looked they could see no sign of any ring!

'Let's go and ask Chinky to help,' said Mollie. So they ran back to the playroom. Chinky was sitting reading. They told him how they had hunted for the ring.

'I'll soon find out if it's in the garden,' he said, shutting his book. 'Is your mother certain she dropped it there?'

'Quite certain,' said Peter. 'How are you going to find out where it is, Chinky?'

'You'll see in a minute!' said the pixie, with a grin. He went to the door of the playroom and looked round. There was no one about. He whistled softly a strange little twittering tune. A freckled thrush flew down to his hand and stood on his out-stretched fingers.

'Listen, Freckles,' said Chinky. 'There is a ring lost in this garden. Get all the birds together and tell them to hunt for it.'

Freckles gave a chirrup and flew off. In a few minutes all the birds in the garden were gathered together in a thick lilac bush. Mollie and Peter could hear the thrush singing away, just as if he were telling a story in a song. They knew he must be telling the birds what to do.

In a few seconds every sparrow, starling, thrush, blackbird, robin, and finch was hopping about the ground, under bushes and in the beds, under the hedges and over the grass. They pecked here and there, they turned over every leaf, and they hunted for that ring as neither Mollie nor Peter could possibly have hunted.

At last Freckles the thrush came back. He flew down on to Chinky's shoulder and chirruped a long and pretty song in his ear. Then he flew off.

'What does he say?' asked Mollie.

'He says that your mother's ring is nowhere here at all,' said Chinky. 'She can't have dropped it in the garden.'

'But she knows she *did*,' said Mollie.

'Well, some one must have found it already, then,' said Chinky. 'I wonder if any goblin was about last night! They are not honest if they find any beautiful jewel. Wait! I'll find out!'

He went to the lawn near the playroom. It was well hidden from the house, so he could not be seen. He drew a ring on the grass in blue chalk.

'Keep away from this ring,' he said to the watching children. 'When I say the goblin spell, you will see blue flames and smoke come up from the ring if the goblins have been this way during the last few hours. Don't go too near. If nothing happens we shall know that no goblins have been this way.'

Mollie and Peter watched whilst Chinky danced slowly round the ring, chanting a string of curious, magic-sounding words.

'Look! Look! Smoke is coming – and blue flames!' shrieked Mollie excitedly. 'Oh, Chinky, don't go too near!'

Sure enough, as they watched, the ring began to smoke as if it were on fire, and small blue flames flickered all around. Chinky stopped singing. He threw a pinch of dust over the ring. Smoke, flames, and chalk ring vanished as if they had never been there!

'Yes,' said Chinky, 'a goblin has been here all right! When a blue chalk ring flames like that it's a sure sign of goblins. I wonder which one it was. I'll just go and ask the fairies at the bottom of the garden – they'll know.'

He ran off. The children didn't follow, for they knew that Chinky didn't like them to see the fairies, who were very shy. He came back, running fast, his face red with excitement.

'Yes – the fairies saw Big-Ears the goblin pass by here last night – so he must have found the ring and taken it. They said that he seemed very pleased about something.'

'Oh dear! How can we get it back for Mother?' asked Mollie in despair.

'We'll get it back all right. Don't worry,' said Chinky. 'As soon as the wishing-chair grows its wings again we'll go off to old Big-Ears. He'll soon give it back. He's an old coward.'

'Good!' said the children in delight. 'Oh, won't it be fun to have an adventure again! Where does Big-Ears live?'

'Not very far away,' said Chinky. 'In Goblin Town. Listen – there's your dinner-bell. You go in to dinner and I'll see if I can get the wishing-chair to grow its wings again. Sometimes a little singing helps it.'

The children ran indoors, bubbling with excitement. What fun if the chair grew its wings that afternoon.

After dinner they ran back to their playroom. Chinky met them at the door with a grin.

'The chair's grown its wings!' he said. 'It is in a great hurry to get away, so come on!'

Peter and Mollie ran into the playroom. The wishing-chair certainly seemed in a great hurry to go. Its wings were flapping merrily, and it was giving little hops about the floor.

'It thinks it's a bird or something!' said Chinky, grinning. 'It will twitter soon!'

The children sat down on the seat. Chinky climbed on to the back. 'To Goblin Town!' he cried.

The chair rose into the air and flew out of the door with such a rush that the children were nearly thrown out of their seats.

'Steady, chair, steady!' said Chinky. 'There's not such a dreadful hurry, you know.'

The chair flew so high in the air that the children were above the clouds, and could see nothing below them but the rolling white mist, like a great dazzling snowfield.

'Where are we now?' asked Mollie, peering down. 'Are we getting near Goblin Town?'

'We must be,' said Chinky. 'But we shan't know till the chair dives down through the clouds again. Ah! Here we go!'

Down went the chair through the cold white

clouds. The children looked to see if Goblin Town was below.

'Look at those funny, crooked little houses!' cried Mollie in delight. 'And look at the goblins! Oh, it's a market, or something!'

The chair flew down to a busy market-place. The goblins crowded round it in surprise.

'Good-afternoon,' said Chinky, getting down from the back of the chair. 'Can you tell me where Big-Ears lives?'

'He lives in the yellow cottage at the foot of the hill,' said a little green goblin, pointing. The children carried the chair down the hill, for it had stopped flappings its wings and seemed tired. They came to the yellow cottage, and Chinky knocked loudly.

The door opened. There stood a goblin with yellow eyes and great big pointed ears that stuck above the top of his head.

'Good-morning, Big-Ears,' said Chinky. 'We have come for that ring you picked up in our garden the other night.

'W-w-w-what r-r-r-ring?' stammered the goblin, going pale with fright. 'I d-d-d-didn't see any ring.'

'Oh yes, you did,' said Chinky firmly. 'And if you don't give it back AT ONCE I'll turn you into a wriggling worm.'

'No, no, no!' cried Big-Ears, falling to his knees. 'Don't do that. Yes – I did take the ring – but I have given it to the Snoogle, who lives in the castle over there.'

'Off to the Snoogle then!' shouted Chinky, and he jumped into the wishing-chair. The children followed – and up went the chair into the air. They were off to the Snoogle – whatever he might be!

CHAPTER THIRTEEN

THE SNOOGLE

The wishing-chair was off to find the Snoogle!

'If the Snoogle has your mother's ring, we shall have to find some way of getting it back,' said Chinky. 'I wonder who or what he is. I've never heard of him before.'

The chair flew on. Soon, in the distance, the three could see an enormous castle set on a hill-top. At the bottom, all round the foot, was a great moat full of water. A drawbridge stretched across the moat – but, even as the children looked at it, it was drawn up into the gateway on the castle side of the moat.

'There's no way of getting in the Snoogle's castle except by flying, that's plain,' said Chinky. 'Fly on to the roof, wishing-chair.'

The wishing-chair flew to the roof of the castle. It was turreted, and the chair flew over the turrets and down on to a flat part behind.

Sitting on the roof basking in the sunshine was the Snoogle.

The children stared at him in astonishment. He was the funniest-looking creature they had ever seen. He had the body of a dragon, the tail of a

cat always twirling and twisting, and the head of a yellow duck!

He was sitting in a deck-chair fast asleep. The wishing-chair flew down beside his chair, and the children stared at the Snoogle. They did not get out of the chair, because, really, they hardly liked the look of the Snoogle. But Chinky jumped down and went to have a good stare at him.

'Snore-r-r-r-r-r!' went the sleeping Snoogle. 'Snore-r-r-r-r-r!'

'Hie! Wake up, Snoogle!' shouted Chinky, and he gave the Snoogle a poke in the chest. The Snoogle woke up in a fright and quacked loudly.

'Quack, quack, quack, quack, quack!' He leapt to his two pairs of dragon feet and glared at Chinky.

'I've come to fetch the ring that Big-Ears the goblin gave you,' said Chinky boldly. 'Will you get it, please?'

'You'd better get it youreslf,' said the Snoogle sulkily.

'Where is it, then?' asked Chinky.

'Go down the stairs there, and walk down two hundred steps,' said Snoogle. 'You will come to a bolted door. Unbolt it and walk in. You will see my bedroom there. In a big box on the mantelpiece you will find the ring. It was given to me by Big-Ears, and I think you should give me something in return for it.'

'You shall have nothing!' cried Chinky. 'You knew quite well that Big-Ears should not have taken that ring from our garden. I believe you were just keeping it for him till people had forgotten it and had given up hunting for it. You are just as dishonest as Big-Ears!'

The Snoogle waved its cat-like tail to and fro in anger. It gave a few loud quacks, but Chinky only laughed. He didn't seem a bit afraid of the Snoogle.

'I'll go down and get the ring,' he said to the others. 'Stay here.'

He ran down the steps – but no sooner had he disappeared down them than the Snoogle also went down – following softly behind Chinky.

'Oh! He's gone to catch Chinky!' cried Mollie. 'Shout, Peter; shout, and warn him!'

So Peter shouted with all his might – but Chinky was too far down the steps to hear. The Snoogle waited for him to unbolt the bedroom door – and then, when Chinky was safely inside looking for the box on the mantelpiece, he slammed the door and bolted it.

'Quack!' he cried, with a deep chuckle. 'Now you are caught, you cheeky little pixie.'

Mollie and Peter were running down the steps, shouting to Chinky. They suddenly heard the sound of the bedroom door being slammed, and the bolts driven home.

'Stop, Mollie,' said Peter, clutching hold of her arm. 'Chinky is caught. It's no use us running straight into the Snoogle as he comes back. Slip into this room here, and perhaps he will go past us up to the roof again.'

They slipped into a nearby room. They hid behind the door – and as he passed, the Snoogle popped his head into the room and looked round it – but he did not see the two children squeezed tightly behind the door.

'Quack!' he said loudly, and went on up the steps.

Mollie and Peter slipped out of the room as soon as it was safe and ran to where Chinky was hammering on the inside of the bolted door in a furious rage. 'Let me out, let me out!' he was shouting.

'Chinky, Chinky, hush!' said Peter. 'We're just going to unbolt the door.'

The bolts were big and heavy. It took both Mollie and Peter to pull them back. They opened the door – and there was Chinky, looking as angry as could be.

'To think I should have been trapped so easily!' said Chinky, in a fury. 'Anyway – I've got the ring! Look!'

He showed them a ring – and sure enough it was the very one their mother had lost! Mollie and Peter were so pleased.

'Now I'll just go and tell that Snoogle what I think of him!' said Chinky fiercely. '*I'm* not afraid of any Snoogle – silly, duck-headed creature!'

'Oh, Chinky, do be careful,' said Mollie, half afraid. 'We've got the ring. Can't we just go quietly up to the roof, get into our chair, and go away? I'd much rather do that.'

'We'll get into the chair and fly away all right,' said Chinky. 'But I'm just going to tell the Snoogle a few things first.'

The children had never seen the little pixie look so angry. He marched up the steps and out on the roof. Mollie and Peter followed.

The Snoogle was looking all round for the two

children, quacking angrily. He was surprised to see them coming up the steps – and even more surprised to see Chinky, whom he thought was safely bolted in the room below.

'Now, look here, Snoogle,' said Chinky boldly, walking right up to the surprised creature, 'how *dare* you try to capture me like that? I am a pixie – yes, and a powerful one too. I can do spells that would frighten you. Shall I turn you into a black-beetle – or a tadpole – or a wasp without a sting?'

To the children's surprise, the Snoogle looked very much frightened. He was such a big creature compared with Chinky – it seemed strange that he should be so scared of him.

'I've a good mind to fly off in our chair to the Pixie King and complain of you,' said Chinky. 'You will have your castle taken away from you then, for daring to interfere with a pixie.'

'No one can get me out of my castle,' said the Snoogle, in a quacking sort of voice. 'I have a big moat round – and a drawbridge that I can keep drawn up for months on end. Do your worst, stupid little pixie!'

'Very well, then, I will!' said Chinky. 'But just to go on with – take that, you silly Snoogle!'

Chinky took hold of the Snoogle's waving tail and pulled it hard. Naughty Chinky! There was no need to do a thing like that. It made the Snoogle very angry indeed ... but he did not dare to touch

Chinky or the children, for he really was afraid of Chinky's magic.

But the Snoogle was not afraid of the wishing-chair. He ran to it and stood by it. 'You shall not fly off in your chair now!' he quacked loudly. 'Aha! That will punish you.'

'Oh yes, we will!' shouted Chinky, and he ran to push the Snoogle away – but, oh dear, oh dear, whatever do you suppose the Snoogle did? With four hard pecks he pecked off the red wings of the poor wishing-chair! There they lay on the ground, four bunches of red feathers!

'Oh! You wicked creature!' shouted Mollie, in a rage. 'You have spoilt our lovely, lovely wishing-chair! Oh, how could you do a thing like that! Oh, Chinky, why did you make the Snoogle angry? Look what he's done!'

Mollie burst into tears. She couldn't bear to see the wings of the wishing-chair on the ground, instead of flapping away merrily on its legs. Peter turned pale. He did not know how they would get home now.

Chinky was full of horror. He had not thought that such a thing would happen – but it was done now!

'Well, I think you'll agree that you can't fly away now,' said the Snoogle, with a grin. 'Take your chair and go down into the kitchen. You can live there now. No one ever comes here – and you can't get out — so we shall be nice company for one another!'

Chinky picked up the chair. The three of them walked down the steps very sorrowfully.

'We are in a pretty fix now!' said Peter gloomily. 'I don't know what we are going to do now that our wishing-chair can't fly!'

CHAPTER FOURTEEN

THE SNOOGLE'S CASTLE

The children and Chinky carried the wishing-chair down to the Snoogle's kitchen. This was a big bare stone place with a huge fire roaring in the grate.

Chinky stood the chair down on the stone floor and sat in it, looking very gloomy.

'I know it was my fault that the wishing-chair's wings were pecked off,' he said to the others. 'Don't cry, Mollie. There must be some way of getting out of the Snoogle's castle.'

'I'm not crying because I'm afraid we can't escape,' said Mollie. 'I'm crying because of the poor wishing-chair. Is this the end of all our flying adventures? It is horrid to think we may never go any more!'

'Don't think about that,' said Chinky. 'The first thing is – can we possibly get out of here? Where is the Snoogle, I wonder?'

'Here!' said the quacking voice of the duck-headed Snoogle, and he looked into the kitchen. 'If you want any tea, there are cakes in the larder – and you might make some tea and put some cakes on a plate for me too.'

'I suppose we might as well do what he says,'

said Peter. He went to the larder and looked inside. He saw a tin there with CAKES printed on it.

Inside there were some fine chocolate buns. The children put some on a plate for themselves and some on a plate for the Snoogle. Mollie put the kettle on the fire to boil. They all waited for the steam to come out – but nobody said a word. They were too unhappy.

When the kettle boiled Mollie made tea in two teapots. She took one teapot, cup and saucer, and plate of cakes to the Snoogle, who was sitting in the dining-room reading a newspaper. It was upside down, so Mollie didn't think it was much use to him. But she was too polite to say so. She couldn't help feeling, too, that it would be much better for all of them if they tried to be friendly with the Snoogle.

She put the tray down by the Snoogle and left him. He opened his great beak before she was out of the room, and gobbled up one cake after another. Mollie thought he must be a very greedy creature.

She went back to the kitchen, and she and the others munched chocolate buns and drank hot tea, wondering gloomily what to do next.

'Perhaps we could swim across that moat,' said Mollie at last.

'We'll look and see, when we can creep away for a few minutes,' said Peter.

'Listen,' said Chinky. 'What's that noise?'

'Snore-r-r-r-r-r! Snore-r-r-r-r-r!' went the Snoogle in the dining-room. The three looked at one another.

'What about poking all round to see if there's any way of escape now?' whispered Peter.

'Come on, then!' said Chinky. They all got up. They went to the kitchen door and opened it. It looked straight on to the moat. How wide and deep and cold it looked!

'Ooh!' said Mollie. 'I'd never be able to swim across that, I'm sure. Nor would you, Peter!'

'And look!' said Chinky, pointing down into the water. 'There are giant frogs there – they would bite us, I expect!'

Sure enough, as Mollie and Peter peered down into the water they saw the blunt snouts of many giant frogs. 'Oooh!' said Mollie. 'I'm not going to jump in there!'

'I say!' said Peter. 'What about the drawbridge? Couldn't we let that down ourselves and escape that way?'

'Of course!' said Chinky. 'Come on. We'll find it before the old Snoogle awakes.'

They went through the kitchen and into a big wide hall. They swung open the great front door. A path led down to a gateway that overlooked the moat. The door of the gateway was the drawbridge, drawn up over the entrance.

The three ran down to the gate. Chinky looked

carefully at the chains that held up the drawbridge.

'Look!' he said to the others. 'These chains are fastened by a padlock. The drawbridge cannot be let down unless the key it fitted into the padlock and the lock is turned. Then the drawbridge will be let down over the moat.'

'Where is the key to the padlock, I wonder,' said Mollie.

'I know,' said Peter. 'The Snoogle has it. I saw a big key hanging from him somewhere.'

'Can't we get it?' asked Mollie. 'He's asleep. Let's try.'

They tiptoed into the dining-room. The Snoogle was certainly very fast asleep.

'I guess we can get the key without waking him!' whispered Chinky, in delight. 'Where is it?'

They looked all round the Snoogle for the key – but they couldn't se it. And then, at last, Peter saw it – or part of it. The Snoogle was sitting on it! They could just see the head of the key sticking out from underneath him.

'No good,' said Chinky, shaking his head and tip-toeing out. 'We should certainly wake him if we tried to pull that key out, as he's sitting on it. I suppose that's why he sat on it, to stop us getting it!'

'Anyway, I expect the drawbridge would have made an awful noise rattling down on its chains,' stid Peter gloomily. 'The Snoogle would have heard it and woken up and come after us.'

'What shall we do now?' said Mollie, in despair. 'We can't swim the moat. We can't unlock the drawbridge and let it down.'

'There's one thing we might try,' said Chinky. 'I might try to whistle one of the birds down to a windowsill and tell it of our dreadful fix. It would fly back to pixie-land and perhaps the King would send to rescue us. You never know.'

'Yes – do that,' said Mollie, cheering up. The children and the pixie went up the stairs and into a bedroom. They leaned out of the open window.

Below lay the silvery moat.

Chinky began to whistle. It was a soft whistle, but a very piercing one. Mollie felt sure that if she had been a bird she would have come in answer to Chinky's whistle.

Chinky stopped his whistling. He looked anxiously into the sky and waited. No bird came. No bird was to be seen.

'I'll try again,' said Chinky. He whistled once more. They waited, looking everywhere for the sign of a bird.

'There are no birds in this Snoogle country,' said the pixie, with a sigh. 'One would have come if it could.'

'Well,' said Mollie, looking worried, 'whatever can we do now? There doesn't seem to be any way of escape at all – nor any way of getting people to help us.'

'Let's go into each of the rooms, upstairs, and downstairs, and see if there is any one there,' said Chinky. 'We might find a servant or some one – they might help us. You never know!'

So the children and the pixie went into each room, one by one. They were queer, untidy rooms. It looked as if the Snoogle lived in one for a bit and then, when it became too untidy, went into another one and lived there until the same thing happened!

There was no one at all in any of the rooms.

Only the Snoogle lived in the castle, that was plain.

'Well, we've been in many fixes,' said the pixie gloomily, 'but this is about the tightest fix we've ever been in. How I hate the Snoogle for pecking the wings off our dear old wishing-chair!'

The children and Chinky went down into the kitchen again. The Snoogle was no longer snoring in the dining-room. He must be awake!

He was. He came into the kitchen, snapping his duck-beak and waving his cat's tail.

'Well,' he said, with a grin. 'Been all over the castle to find a way of escape? Aha! You won't find that in a hurry! Well, as you're here, you may as well wait on me. I'm tired of doing my own cooking and washing-up. You can do it for me.'

'We won't then!' said Peter furiously. 'It is bad enough to have to be here, without waiting on a duck-headed creature like you!'

'Hush, Peter,' said Mollie suddenly. 'Hush! Very well, Snoogle, we will do as you say. Where would you like your supper? There is a cloth in the drawer, but it is dirty. Have you a clean one, so that I can begin to get your supper for you?'

'You are a sensible girl,' said the Snoogle, pleased. 'I have a clean cloth upstairs. I will get it.'

He went out of the room. Chinky and Peter turned and stared at Mollie in amazement. What did she mean by giving in so meekly to the horrid Snoogle?

'Peter! Chinky! Look!' said Mollie, and she pointed to the wishing-chair, where it stood in a corner of the kitchen. The others looked – and whatever do you suppose they saw? Guess?

The wishing-chair was growing new wings! Yes, really! Tiny red buds were forming on its legs. They grew fast. They burst into feathers. They were growing into new, strong wings!

'Goodness!' said Peter and Chinky, amazed. 'Who would have thought of that! Good old wishing-chair!'

'Quick – here comes the Snoogle. Put the chair behind the table, where he can't see its wings growing,' said Mollie. So Chinky pushed it behind the table just in time. The Snoogle pattered in, and held out a clean cloth to Mollie.

'Thank you,' said the little girl politely. 'And have you got some egg-cups, please? I will boil you some eggs for supper.'

The Snoogle trotted out to fetch some egg-cups. As soon as he was gone, Mollie, Peter, and Chinky crowded into the wishing-chair.

'Home, as quickly as you can, wishing-chair!' shouted Chinky. The chair flapped its new red wings and rose into the air. The Snoogle came running into the kitchen. He quacked with rage. He tried to get hold of the chair as it flew past him.

Chinky kicked out at him and caught him on his big yellow beak. The Snoogle gave a squawk and sat down suddenly.

'Good-bye, good-bye, dear Snoogle!' yelled
Chinky, waving his hand. '*Do* call in and see us
when you are passing, and we'll give you a clean
cloth for tea and boil you some eggs!'

The chair flew home at a great rate. At last it
came to the playroom and flew into it. It set itself
down on the floor, and its wings gave one more flap
and vanished.

'Ha! The old wishing-chair is tired!' said
Chinky. 'I don't wonder! I hope it will soon grow
its wings again. We do have some adventures,
don't we, children!'

'Where's Mother's ring, Chinky?' asked Peter,
suddenly remembering why they had gone adventuring – to get his mother's lost ring!

'Here you are,' said Chinky, and he gave Peter
the ring. 'Won't your Mother be pleased! She
won't guess what a lot of adventures we had getting
back her ring for her!'

Peter and Mollie ran off happily. They called
their mother and gave her her ring. 'You *had* dropped it in the garden, Mother,' said Peter.

'Thank you! You *are* kind children to find it for
me!' said Mother. But she didn't guess that Big-
Ears the goblin had stolen it – and that the Snoogle
had had it too! No – that was the children's secret.